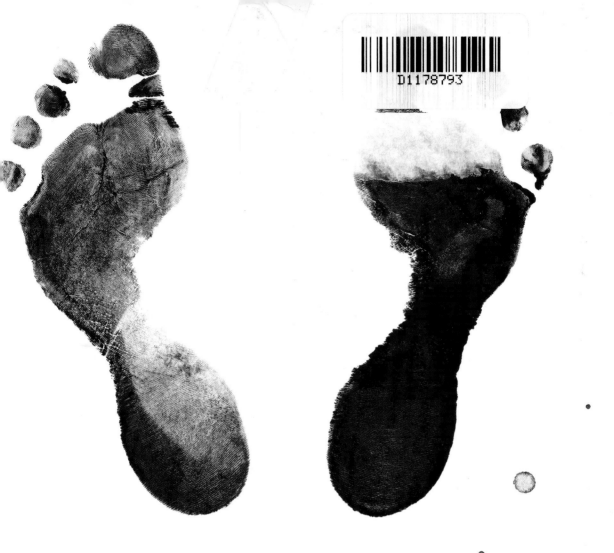

Jake's feet

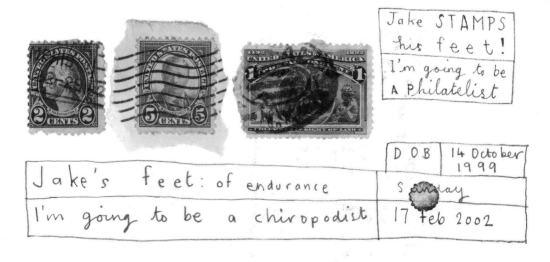

Jake STAMPS his feet! I'm going to be A Philatelist

Jake's feet: of endurance	DOB	14 October 1999
	Sunday	
I'm going to be a chiropodist	17 feb 2002	

12 inches = 1 foot
3 feet = 1 yard. → PRACTICE BASKETBALL in your backyard.

HB

1 2 3 4

3B   Blue   2B   Red HB   B   2B
        HB

GROW UP

Sandy Turner

![Walker Books bear logo]

WALKER BOOKS
AND SUBSIDIARIES
LONDON • BOSTON • SYDNEY

First published 2003 in the USA by Joanna Cotler Books
Published 2003 in Great Britain by Walker Books Ltd
87 Vauxhall Walk, London SE11 5HJ
2 4 6 8 10 9 7 5 3 1
© 2003 Sandy Turner
Manufactured in China   All rights reserved
British Library Cataloguing in Publication Data:
a catalogue record for this book is available
from the British Library
ISBN 0-7445-8666-6

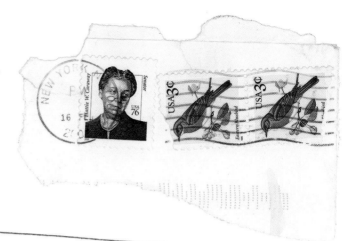

I'M going to be GREEN - FINGERED: (a gardener

palm tree?

START

FINISH

FOR BILL

 and ELEANOR and LYDIA and BLANCHE x
not forgetting Jake

WHAT ARE you going TO BE WHEN YOU GROW UP? THE GROWN-UP ASKED THE CHILD.

I don't know,

said the CHILD . . . . A NURSE ?

ooh... I know
I'm going to be a . . .

SPLASH

I'm going to be a
SCIENTIST

I'm going to be a
DENTIST

I'm going to be a
HYPNOTIST

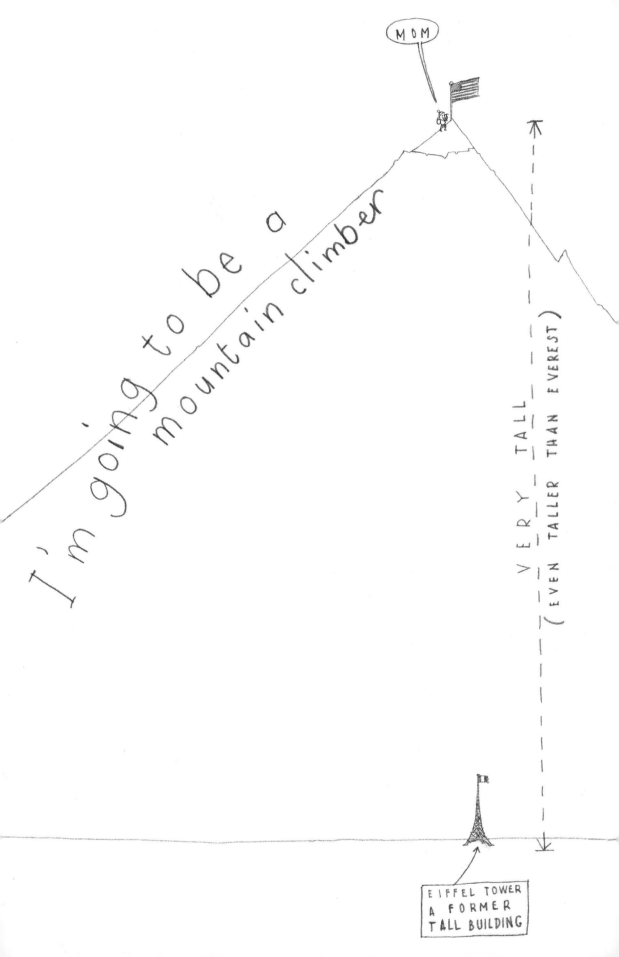

OR I MIGHT BE

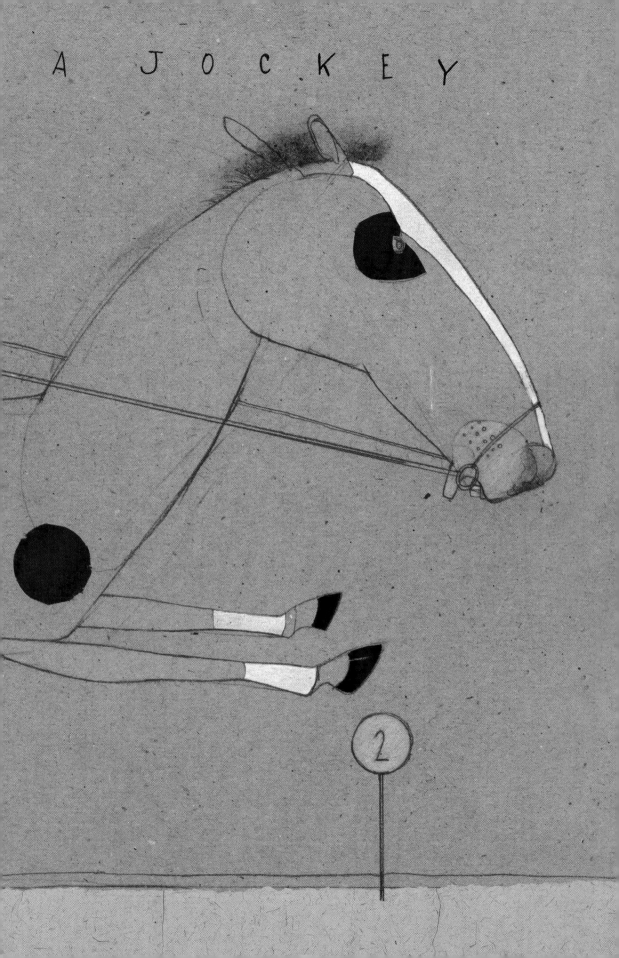

I'M GOING TO BE
A WINDOW CLEANER

AN ASTRONOMER

A MAGICIAN

OR EVEN A LION TAMER

OR A TICKET COLLECTOR

I'm going to play the SAXOPHONE

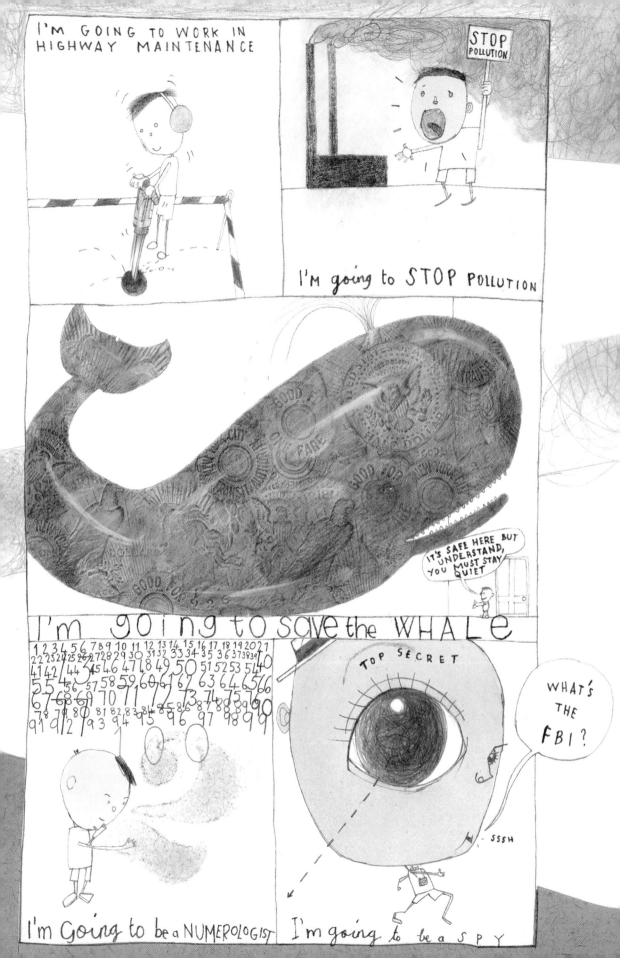

NEW YORK
JUL 19 '01
NY

U.S. POSTAGE
$ 0.80

LENNY LIGHTHOUSE, ESQ.
CAPE COD
FISHBONE County

I'm going to deliver the U.S. mail.

I might be a
LIGHTHOUSE
KEEPER

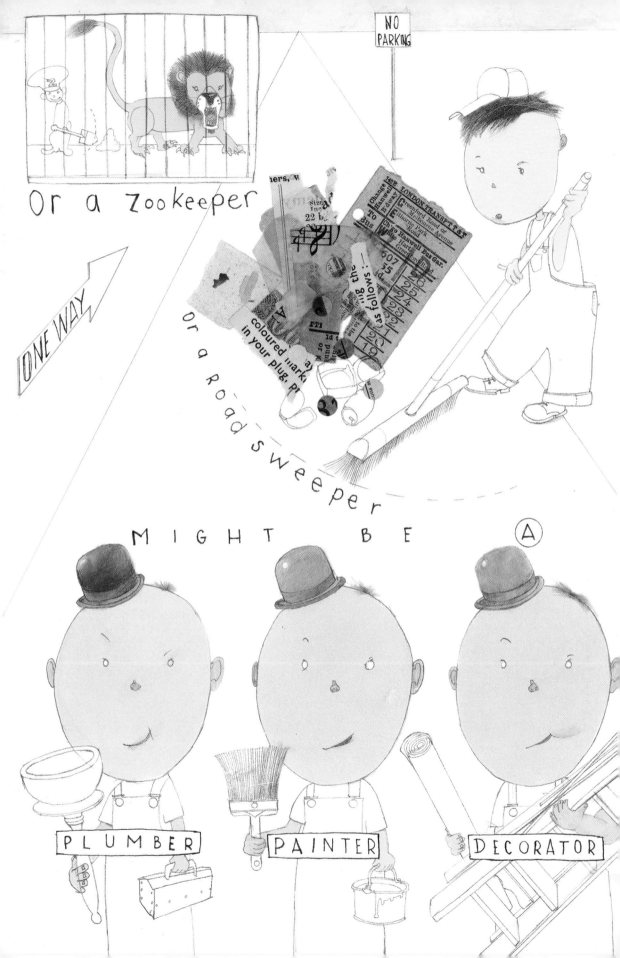

Or a zookeeper

ONE WAY

NO PARKING

Or a road sweeper

MIGHT BE (A)

PLUMBER

PAINTER

DECORATOR

or an ∘ UNDERTAKER ∘

I might be

Could work on a FERRY
going to be an ARCHITECT:
OR I might fly a JET

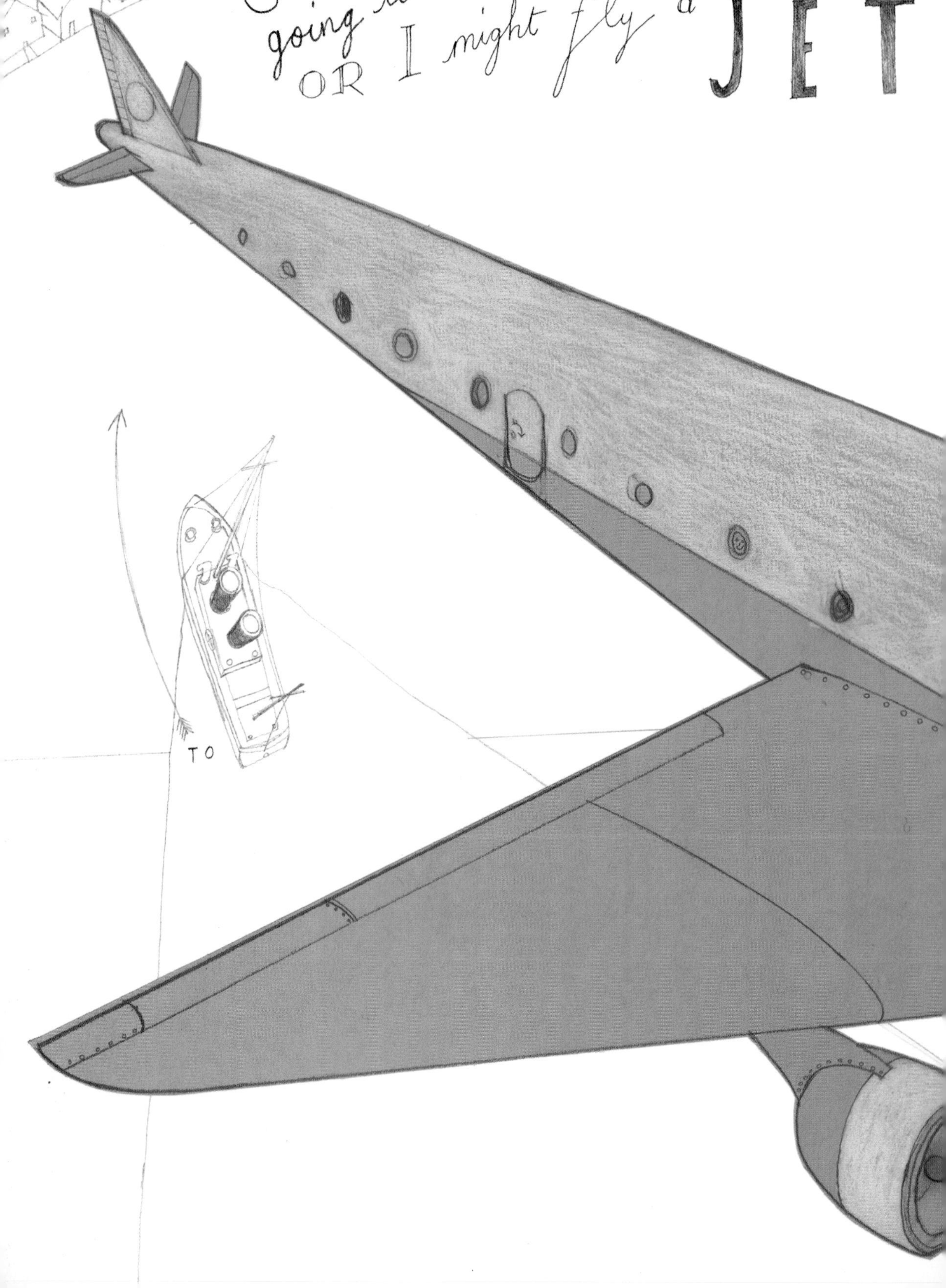

TO

I'm going to COMMAND A FLEET of SUBMARINES

and FRO

BATTERIES NOT INCLUDED

I'm going to grow

TALLER

I am going to be the

7' 7"

23

BASKETBALLER.

And the grown-up said

YOU HAD

better

EAT UP

your

GREENS.

How To be an ARTIST:

draw around your hand.

place hand palm side down on the paper. Spread
your fingers evenly. Carefully ~~draw~~ draw round the
edges. Like tracing. Lift your hand away
an' bINGO there is an actual outline of your
HAND.   Add detail, color in.

4

3

5

2

BIG Hand

1

START

older

HANDSome